The stories in *AM/PM* have ruined me as a reader of shorts. I will no longer be satisfied by the merely beautiful, the singularly clever, or the one big thought purely rendered. I want all those things in a two-hundred–word package. I want to be highly amused and deeply sad at the exact same time. Amelia Gray packs more power in a paragraph than I thought possible.

—Stacey Swann, Editor of *American Short Fiction*

a book by amelia gray

*f*eatherproof BOOKS

Illustration: zachdodson.com

Published by
featherproof books
Chicago, Illinois
www.featherproof.com

First Edition

∞

Library of Congress Control Number: 2008940498

ISBN: 0-9771992-7-4
ISBN 13: 978-0-9771992-7-3

Set in Archer

Printed in the United States of America

AM/PM

amelia gray

For Jon: this book is a symbol.

Terrence cannot think of a job position with more weight in the title than lifeguard. "Firefighter" simply describes. "Pastor" makes little sense, outside of a treatment for meat in Mexico. Usually pork. However, "lifeguard" carries with it a great deal of gravity which many might consider unearned by the lanky youths typically found atop most lifeguard stands. Terrence offers himself as a humble exception to the rule: out of shape and in full awareness of the importance of his position.

Three bathers prepare to enter the water. Terrence watches very closely from his stand, his red rescue buoy strapped across his lap. They are three women in thick one-piece suits. The pocked texture on their upper thighs is visible from fifty feet. They hold hands like girls and jump, shrieking, and Terrence holds his breath with them until all three surface, blissfully unaware of the risks they take when they place their blind faith in that water.

15:PM

There is a poetry to the wasted life, but little beauty. The poetry to an empty bed is beauty, Charles recognizes, and there is a poetry to the second hand on a clock, which is a kind of beauty, but the only beauty in the wasted life is of efficiency, and grace, and a complete knowledge of a small portion of the world. Charles recognizes the grace of a trip to the store. He feels the efficiency in slipping the same type of milk into the same place in the refrigerator door, between the pickles and the mayonnaise. Charles accepts the knowledge of the second hand.

Remain Healthy All Day: Drink a spoonful of oil every morning. Reach up with your arms and extend your body to its full height. Use a warm towel to dry the cat. Consider a philosophical idea larger than your area of expertise. Avoid getting cancer. Chalk up bad decisions to outside influences. Don't take your father too seriously. Play a game where you close your eyes very tightly, and when you open your eyes, you have amnesia and you must draw the details of your life from your surroundings. Give up smoking, drinking, and poetic verse. Remind yourself how important you are to your friends or at least your animals. Wax the floor in socks. Enter into a healthy, monogamous relationship. Consider briefly the idea of a soulmate. Light an entire box of matches and throw it into the sink. Hold a metal rod to the heavens and beg for whatever comes next.

17:PM

In the event that Reginald caught her on her way out, Olivia had prepared a speech:

Don't think for an instant that you've escaped detection. I saw you looking at those advertisements for used bookshelves like we had in college. I saw you examining the bottom shelf at the liquor store for scotch in a plastic jug. You will not get us ejected from the theater with your rowdiness. You will not shave your beard and hide my brassieres. You will not cause mischief at the furniture store, and come home worried that they'll take your job. You're the owner, for heaven's sake. If you would like to reclaim your youth, sleep with a sales girl and buy another car. It pains me to see you this way, and it makes me tired.

He slept through her exit. When she returned, he was still asleep. She woke him and helped him prepare for his bath.

AM:18

Charles knew what that look meant. It meant that Doreen disapproved and was playing at being offended, but if the line of inquiry continued, she would actually be offended. She had leveled that look at him in kitchens, crowded bars, in the game rooms of friends' houses. Charles couldn't get away from it. He could charter a plane, fly to an empty continent and wade ashore, only to find Doreen standing there, holding the guts of his plane's navigational system like some righteous nun, giving him that look.

19:PM

Hazel and Tess each bought a flavored water and sat on the stoop in front of the market.

Tess was talking about the previous night, her first date with a man named Wallace. "We talked about flying," she said.

"And he's afraid of it, too?"

"Not at all. And his parents were both in crashes."

"That doesn't bother him?"

"They called and said, 'Hey, buddy, we're in Costa Rica, and guess what just happened.'"

Hazel took a long drink of water. "Weird," she said.

"He loves his parents, of course."

"That's a good sign."

"He made sure to mention that he loves his parents. They called from Costa Rica, and he wouldn't have known otherwise, since it wasn't on the news. Everyone was okay."

"You mean, everyone survived? No fatalities?"

"Everyone walked away, except one stewardess who burned her foot on the fuselage."

"That's different, then."

Tess got up and tossed her empty bottle into the garbage. "It was a crash," she said. "People could have perished. Sorry to disappoint."

"Don't take that tone," Hazel said, standing.

AM:2Ø

Good morning, John Mayer Concert Tee! I'm happy to see you survived the night. I know that I said my vespers before I pulled the covers up over my lips and nose to minimize the mosquito exposure. I looked to my dresser in the dark and added a silent refrain that you, John Mayer Concert Tee, would emerge, unscathed, from that land of broken windows. That your soft-pilled black poly blend, proudly emblazoned with the two-tone visage of Mr. Mayer himself, would not be spirited away. It is morning, John Mayer Concert Tee. I have a series of problems that cannot be solved.

21:PM

The neighbors were fighting in the street again, really screaming this time, and Simon was writing it all down.

"I'm worried they'll wake the baby," Betty said. "You think you're the next Carver."

"Yes, that's what I think." He was lying belly-down on the bed with his head halfway out the window like he was about to take a flying leap, like he was Superman.

"Superman would go out and save them. Carver, too."

"Carver wouldn't get up to sharpen a pencil," Simon said. "He'd get a good woman to do it. And Superman would recognize that that girl out there is holding her own well enough and doesn't require saving."

"He's screaming at her."

"She's translating his language."

"I'd call the police if you started screaming at me."

Simon shrugged, writing. "Different language," he said. "Lost in translation."

"Bill Murray'd save her, too."

The neighbors stopped fighting so abruptly that Simon and Betty both leaned toward the window.

From the silence, Simon: "Bill Murray'd save her eight bucks and tell her how *Superman* ends."

June was the kind of woman who not only talked to her cats, but consulted them seriously about world affairs and life changes. *Mister Pickles,* she would say in that adorable voice women reserve for their cats and when they want a large favor performed, *Mister Pickles, what is your opinion on the recent World Bank shake up? Do you feel that man should be fired? All he wanted to do was to make his girlfriend happy.* The cat would look up at her, thinking for one wild moment that the tendrils of hair around her face were lizard tails.

23:PM

The girls, for all their tea-time advice, were each unhappy in their own relationships. Missy and her new husband fought constantly, and Chastity had left the father of her child to go on a spiritual journey. Frances had no prospects and a house full of fleas. She scratched a flea bite on her ankle with the heel of her shoe.

"They're all intimidated by you," Missy said. "They're intimidated by the fact that a girl as young as you, excuse me, could be so sophisticated and beautiful and great."

"They're not sophisticated," Chastity said.

Having a flea bite made Frances feel fleas everywhere. She dug her hands into her hair, scratching her scalp. She had said a few months ago that she'd never had a flea bite, which was how these things happened.

"Not at that age," Missy said. "They don't even know how to fake it until at least thirty."

"Men begin at thirty," Chastity said, raising her glass.

"Life starts the day after thirty-five," Frances said. She felt like there was a flea under her arm, where she couldn't look without being conspicuous. Instead, she scratched under her arm.

Missy was watching her. "Are you okay? You look itchy."

"I *am* itchy," Frances said. Her heel had worked its way to her mid-calf. She couldn't say anything about fleas while they were eating. "I'm itching to find a man!"

A couple at another table turned to look. Frances reached under her shirt, scratching her belly.

"That's no way to find a man," the woman said.

Frances glared at the woman. "You stay out of it!"

AM:24

Hazel and Tess were spending an excellent Sunday afternoon trying to decide the best way to die.

"Old age?" Tess suggested.

"Old age is a cop-out," Hazel said. "It's a nice way of saying your organs have sunk so low that you can't summon the strength to reach them. Dying of old age is like being crucified."

"I don't get it."

"Think on it for a while."

Tess didn't like it when Hazel told her to think on things. "Exposure," she said.

"That's a good one, in theory, but what is one truly exposed to, in those last moments?"

"A blizzard, usually."

Hazel gave Tess a look that meant Tess was a few steps behind in the conversation again.

25:PM

Carla switched off the hair dryer. "It's easy to forget how much around us is flammable," she said.

Andrew didn't look up from his dress shirt. "I believe I have a stain," he said.

"We could all go up at any moment."

"The human body is ninety-five percent water."

"That's just the blood," she said, pulling her hair up into a rhinestone-studded clip.

"You're being morbid."

"I'm telling the truth. Bone is only twenty-two percent. Give that a couple days to dry out and you've got yourself a nice little blaze."

He looked at her. "Listen," he said. "I'm sorry."

AM:26

The landscape men trimmed the trees outside Olivia's office window. It was necessary, because the branches were providing easy access for squirrels to the roof.

She watched them remove a series of ash branches, working up to a large one near the top. When the workers cut it, it didn't fall. The remaining branches were thick enough to hold it up and it hung there, suspended, the cut section swinging slowly with the movements of the tree.

27:PM

The man sitting alone smiles when his phone rings. The couple smiles at one another and the woman covers her mouth. A father walks hunched through the parking lot, a newspaper under his arm. He reaches for the child's wrist. The girl touches the car's headlight to hold herself up. Inside, a college student writes in her day planner with a purple pen. A young man takes pictures of himself next to the door. Tess feels that at any moment her heart could stop.

The truck, advertising FISH and MEAT and GOURMET BRANDS, got stuck on the hump between the parking lot and the road in front of the deli next door to our apartment. We went outside because we wanted to count the wheels still touching the ground but the driver waved us away. So we went back inside, where we could only see the back of the truck from the window, and just barely the cars in the street, swerving to avoid it. Somebody said, What would happen if the back end disconnected from the front end, and rolled in through the window and into our home? Killing us all? And causing thousands of dollars of structural damage for our landlord? And somebody else said, I think you have sufficiently answered your own question.

29:PM

Imagine if you could call up all your exes, and bring them together on a basketball court to play a pickup game. Maybe you could also call all the girls you've ever loved, split them into the Girls You Had a Chance With and the Girls You Never Had a Chance With. Have them play shirts and skins. It won't be for your honor, though you'll be the only one watching. You will promise pizza and beer to the winners. The girls you never had a chance with will spit and glare, and the girls you still may have a chance with will snivel and look at you when they make jump shots.

The winners will take your wallet and invite the losers out. Everyone will forget to give you directions, and you'll be left sitting in the gym parking lot.

You'll go home and watch basketball movies. You'll build a makeshift court from scrap lumber in your backyard, and leave messages on all of their answering machines, inviting them back. You'll go out back every night and play H-O-R-S-E, waiting for them to return. You will wear your shirt when you are shirts and you will remove your shirt when you are skins.

AM:3∅

It was still dark, but Terrence's eyes adjusted enough that he could sense the movement of his hand before his face. "Charles," he said. "I believe we are in a small box."

"Indeed," Charles said, from the darkness. Terrence judged him to be about five feet away, but when he reached his arm out, he touched Charles's knee, which startled them both. The knee was cold and hairy. Charles's knee made Terrence more nervous than the existence of the small box.

He leaned back and startled again when he touched the soft walls of the box. The thick velvet felt deep enough to sink his fingers into, but he didn't want to know what was down there and instead let his hand rest on the surface.

Terrence considered the letter he would write to his girlfriend when he was free. He thought fondly of the time they ate cotton candy until she vomited.

31:PM

Tess realized one of the great modern dating sadnesses: everyone is so used to the comforting glow of the computer screen that nobody can go so far as to say "good morning" in public without being liquored up. If ever we do accidentally function as human beings, we call it *instinct*, as in, "sorry about the coffee, or your dress, or my last marriage, but I was operating on instinct," as if it's a failure to behave the way we're all designed. Everyone forgets that acting on instinct has gotten many soldiers through many wars and the rest of us through long lives. The realization caused Tess to paint the dead ladybug on her bedside table with gold frost nail polish, which, as she predicted, did make it look prettier.

Social code was created for the thrill of dragging one's fingertips across the inner thigh of another man's wife. It has been enforced for centuries so that the room will go quiet when the boss is advised to take a flying fuck at a rolling doughnut. The thrill of acting on instinct should never require an apology. An apology would be an act of belittlement; receiving it, an act of humiliation.

The ladybug is not dead: Good-bye, golden friend.

AM:32

By then, the cats were used to the sound of construction next door. Carla hoped it would make the move easier for them, though she anticipated the startled cat noises, the wide eyes and that low groan like the sound a machine makes. This didn't help the prospect of the big move, of course. There were boxes that needed to be opened and checked for contents, and still more boxes that had to be created and filled with the last of it, including perishables, spillables, and the last of the glassware. Packing glassware in secret sounds more stressful than it is. With the newspaper softened by the humid air, it would be easy to wrap and pack her wine glasses without waking Andrew at all.

33:PM

The man who owned the furniture store was really glaring at Martha and Emily by then. They had been testing the stability of his coffee tables by piling on top of them, first Martha on her back and then Emily on her front. The owner thought it was pretty funny at first, but when they kept going and he determined there was no candid camera to catch his reaction, he started pacing back and forth in his glass-walled office.

Emily took Martha's hand and led her over to a three-legged table with a glass top.

"Fall back on it," she said.

"I'm not falling back on it."

"Come on."

"There's no way, under *any* circumstance, that I would fall back on a glass table."

"Heat of the moment."

"No way. I'd have to be on drugs."

"So you're on drugs," Emily said. "So we decide to relive our college days, and you're on drugs, now fall back."

The owner picked up his phone. In the reflection of the glass, Martha could see the two of them, together. They were reliving their college days, and she was on drugs, and it wasn't even going to hurt.

Andrew's problem with women was that he was analytical and they were always, always emotional. Women made fun of him for measuring out salt and spices when he cooked. Even the ones who never cooked would criticize him, leaning against the doorway of the kitchen as if they knew they shouldn't trespass but teasing him anyway. At the movies they smacked him with popcorn buckets for commenting on an incongruous detail while they were building up the stamina to cry. None of it made sense to Andrew. He was very loving, and concerned, and simply knew where to place sadness and fear and anger, so that it could be accessed with great efficiency when necessary.

"It's just you and me, house," Andrew said.

The house was not so sure.

35:PM

With practice, Hazel learned to paint rooms. The evidence could be found in the botched green walls of the room she left and would always remember, even when the house is sold and the room is repainted.

Understand that if you don't paint a room properly, you will know those pieces of wall forever. Understand that every piece of paint not properly applied continues to quietly exist. The misapplied strokes hold a dull truth that remains despite new coats.

AM:36

After a night of terrible sleep, Tess awoke to the realization that cows become meat, though they eat none, and the same goes for vegetarians.

She drank her coffee with extra cream and no sugar. The black linen dress hanging on the wall of the coffee house aspired to belong to a little girl, size six.

A man spoke into a cell phone. He said, Since I met you, baby, I've never been the same.

Another man said to a child, Where are you going, you bug? Don't make me squeeze your little paws, you bug.

37:PM

Unload your perishables and empty boxes. Give away old clothes and broken cookware. Crush the empty cans and load them with the yellow newspapers. Shred the sensitive documents. Discard fingernail clippings. Get rid of those photographs and letters. Offload the old enemies. A lighter life, at any price.

AM:38

When Martha was a girl, fire safety was something presented on public service commercials and school visits from volunteer firemen. They even brought a miniature house, perhaps half the size of the house she grew up in, with child-sized stairs and rooms.

The children crawled into the house and the adults would start the sweet-smelling fog machine and pump it in through the windows and vents and say, Get down, get out, remember your training. Martha would obediently get down and get out, though she liked the way the smoke smelled.

The adults said, You must have a plan, and Martha made a secret plan: in case of fire, she would fill up the bathtub, get in so she would save her pajamas from burning, and simply peek her nose above the water to smell that candy smoke.

39:PM

It was a warm Friday afternoon, and the rain hadn't yet begun. Sam was throwing a rubber-band ball at Hazel's forehead with repeated accuracy.

"I wish you wouldn't do that," Hazel said. She closed her eyes when the rubber-band ball struck her forehead.

"Do you have a better idea?"

"You could *not* do that."

"Sorry," he said, catching the ball and throwing it again in rhythm. "I won't define myself by what I am *not*, and what I *will not* do."

She sighed. "You could throw it at the wall next to my forehead." She kept her forehead still for him when she pointed.

"No go, unfortunately," he said, scooping up the ball. "I place too high a value on human interaction."

"You could throw it at somebody else for a few hours."

Sam looked wounded. He winged it hard enough to leave a red welt between her eyes.

"I'd never do that to you," he said. "I love you."

"Thank you," she said.

"At least we have that," he said, aiming for the welt.

AM:4Ø

After Carla left, Andrew discovered that their house had three secret hiding places. In the second bedroom, he found a small cubby in the upper right corner of the closet, enough room for a medium-sized box or a small child. Under the sink, loose planks covered a few inches of secret space.

At the bottom of the stairs in the entry hall closet was the most exciting secret area. Close inspection revealed a panel that lifted up to expose the underpinnings and pipes of the house. He was shocked he hadn't found the secret earlier.

The space had its own climate. In an emergency, Andrew could possibly fit in the area. This would be an emergency that required not exiting the house through the front door, five feet away. It would be an emergency requiring escape or concealment. The wood around the panel was original to the house, sixty or seventy years old. Andrew felt terribly safe.

41:PM

Charles decided to see if he could live without worldly possessions. He said that giving them up one at a time was the scientific way to do it, which made sense to Doreen because she had bought him a subscription to *Nature* the previous Christmas, and since then he had been fascinated by the scientific method. Doreen's friends suggested that she give him time, then they suggested that she draw the line at items important to her. Her friends made no suggestions at all for one week, when Charles packed their cell phones into the garage. When he brought them out, her voicemail was full of messages saying *This has to stop*.

That night, Doreen watched Charles dismantle the ceiling fan. "This has to stop," she said.

"You only concern yourself with larger things," he said. "You didn't notice the week I went without socks."

"I do your laundry. I notice everything."

"Speaking of, I have the clothes dryer on schedule for next week."

The base of the ceiling fan came down in one piece, and he wrapped the globes carefully with newspaper before unscrewing the blades. He lay them in a neat stack and arranged them all in a box.

"The girls are talking about you again," Doreen said.

"Those women need to learn a thing or two about compromise," Charles said.

He took the ceiling fan away. Doreen looked at the bare wires dangling from the ceiling and wondered how a scientist might see them.

AM:42

Reginald closed down the furniture store on Mondays. He tried not to keep a set schedule on his day of rest, but he was an organized man by nature and did find satisfaction in loose guidelines. Before noon, he would ride his horse across his property. Sometimes he would find the cows, and sometimes he would ride the perimeter, checking the electrified fence. Around noon, Olivia would bring him a cold lunch on the porch. It was often a sandwich made from the leftovers from the previous night, chicken salad made from the dinner cutlets, or meatloaf soaked in ketchup. Olivia gave old meat new life between bread.

To appease her in the evenings, Reginald would fix something small around the house. To show her that he was still vital, he would change the dead bulbs in the foyer chandelier or put new hinges on the driveway gate. At night, he bathed in a bathtub she filled with gallons upon gallons of mineral oil.

43:PM

Olivia dreams that her body becomes pliable enough that she can stretch very thin and cover most of the rooms of the house. Her body is so thin that the bones are clearly visible, and the veins stretch, and the blood has more distance to travel and as a result, the edges of her body are very cold. Reginald opens the front door, removes his shoes, and takes only one step before recoiling in horror at the chilly mass that is Olivia's body, stretched and waiting. In her dreams, she controls every aspect of her life.

They are conduits of emotion, kids are. They're parrots who wear little shoes. The only difference is, when you see a parrot, you never say, gosh, that parrot says the darndest things. You might look at the parrot and say *Polly? Polly?* even when the owner says very clearly to you that the parrot's name is not Polly. You might say to the parrot, *Polly want a cracker? Polly? Why are you wearing little shoes?*

45:PM

They were in love! At night, Carla would read a book and soak her feet in the kitchen sink. Leonard found it charming, and would sometimes kiss her feet when she came to bed. Sometimes there was still soap between her toes, and he cherished the soap and cherished the toes. She would laugh and kick at him playfully and call it a feast of love. If he had nightmares she would praise his fantastic imagination until he slept again and dreamed that he won a highly respected award. He made crepes for lunch, and they would spread butter or chocolate or pesto sauce inside and discuss if savory or sweet was superior. Their discussions often ended with a cavalcade of laughing shoves, and then he'd return again to the feet, kissing the soft pads of her toes while she squealed.

Eventually something wasn't right, and the two moved on, and Carla told her new boyfriends that she'd always thought the foot thing was creepy.

E,

Baby, you give me hives. You're lucky. I happen to think it's an essential function of any relationship that one party be covered in hives at all times. Even in business relationships. Secret hives. You know what I'm talking about.

—M.

47:PM

Just because you made it warm doesn't make it yours: A lesson for felines.

Feline Posits: What if one makes it warm for a long time?

A Response: I will still put it on the towel rack, because it is still a towel.

Feline Posits: What if one conveys pride of ownership via claws?

A Response: Nothing is truly owned, supporting nothing is truly yours.

Feline Posits: What of one's blood, in one's body?

A Response: Blood does not own the body, and body does not own the blood, so says the Rite of Communion.

Feline Posits: What is to become of us, then, and our loneliness?

A Response: Be blessed with the temporary nature of the towel, and of your body.

Doreen sat naked at the table, uploading her photographs. "I have complete control of my cropping area!" she said.

Charles closed the science magazine he had been reading at the breakfast nook. "That's comforting," he said, taking up his tea.

Her black hair was so long by now, it coiled around the base of her chair. She was too lazy to put it up, or had misplaced all of her rubber bands, and it spread out so thick behind her that it looked like she'd grown from it, instead of the other way around.

He watched the hair like it was his wife, and his wife like she was an adornment of her hair, a barrette or peach-colored band. "Would you like a glass of water?" he asked.

"That's strange."

"Water is strange?"

Doreen's hair was bright and soft. She hadn't showered, and the oils gave it a healthy luster. "Once you're married for ten years," she said, "you should start forgetting to ask if I want water." Charles was mesmerized by the way it fell over her shoulders, which were not beautiful, or which were beautiful but not as beautiful as her hair.

"We are among the lucky," Charles said.

49:PM

And may the women hold their brave faces to the sun as the men become afflicted with a terrible pestilence, and may their flesh rain upon the heads of the chosen people. May their hair clog the sewers in the streets, and their broken bodies tumble into the sea! May their useless fury fail to stir the tapestries in the temple, and may the LORD find solace in their swift destruction!

AM:5Ø

Leonard decided that the chaise longue was his favorite piece of furniture and that he would never leave it. We had to bring his soup upstairs, and even then he didn't like to eat, because he was afraid he would drip on the chaise longue. We'd all sit around and talk a little, but none of the chairs in his house were as comfortable, and once Leonard claimed it, it felt strange to sit on it with him. We were closer than we meant to be, even if we were sitting on the far side of the chaise longue. After a while, it felt strange to be in the same room with the two of them.

51:PM

Sam came out of the bathroom glowering, like it was Hazel's fault.

"Feeling better?" Hazel said.

"Coffee hurts when it comes back up."

"I'm sorry, dear."

He sat next to her on the couch, his hands balled into fists. He smacked his lips.

"We should go to breakfast," said Hazel.

Sam looked at her.

massive PDF file is a symbol of my love for you. It is ...aphic and full of information. It takes time to fully load, and when it's running I find it difficult to complete other work. There are parts that I would rather not read, parts I have to read, and parts I'll never read or even know about, but they will always be there. I cannot change the content of this massive PDF file, and I cannot decide when it will begin or end. In fact, it is always there, on my desktop. Even if I put it in my Recycle Bin, it is there, and even if I empty the Recycle Bin it is still there *somewhere*. I would have to powder the hard drive to be rid of all traces of this massive PDF file, which is a symbol of my love for you.

53:PM

Tess felt rather certain that she would die alone. She blamed her arms, which she found to be fatter than normal arms. She blamed her poor body image, which she couldn't seem to shake, even as she got older and found that the girls around her had turned into women, had gotten pregnant and lost their shapes entirely. She took too many pictures of herself and scrutinized them for flaws, and then made copies of the prints and taped them on telephone poles across town with her phone number printed clearly across them.

People called from all over, mostly men, asking about the girl in the photograph. Tess told them, That girl is a runaway, and if you find her, try to keep her in one place and secretly phone the police.

The men said, She looks a little old for a runaway.

Tess said, She's disturbed.

When she went out, Tess was much bolder than usual. She wore sleeveless shirts and made eye contact with the boys at the check-out counter. In the library, she sat at a center table and held her face to the light as she read. Whenever anyone approached her to ask if she had been helped, or if she had read other books by that author, she gathered her things and ran. Nobody could ever see what she was running from.

AM:54

The intense regret of purchasing inexpensive curtains one cannot afford! Feeling doubtful about the idea that suede curtains will make this room look something other than laughable! Panicked financial insecurity, linked closely to a fear of being alone! Sinking emotions related to a worthless mass of completed work! The desire to do all one can to rip off an honest business! The creeping disgust directed toward the cat with worms!

55:PM

"We'll get a babysitter," Betty said, shifting the baby from one arm to the other. "I'll find a restaurant with good lighting."

"Good," said Simon. He was reading a book about organic gardening.

"Lighting is essential," she said.

Gardening, Simon learned, is easiest when you respect the land and the tools you are given.

She was flipping through the phone book, reading carefully for any intimations of weak lighting. "We'll have dinner," she said. "Then, we'll meet up with everyone. What about Italian?"

"Too spicy."

"Cheese isn't spicy."

He shrugged. Planting the proper seeds at the proper times means respecting the land, and the land will bear fruit in answer to your respect. "Indian?" he asked.

She looked at him. "Everything's spicy."

"You have to order a curry," he said. He kissed his fingers, as a gourmand.

Betty shut the phone book and walked into the bedroom. Simon read about winter plants, tubers and flowering squashes.

The power went out during the storm. Hazel and Sam talked in the darkness without touching.

Sam had given up on finding a flashlight and instead lay on the kitchen floor. "Goethe said that everything is metaphor."

"I can never pronounce his name correctly."

"Gerr-tay."

"Gare-tah."

"Gareth."

"Certainly it's not 'Gareth'."

"Certainly not."

A flash of lightning briefly illuminated them both. They listened for the thunder. "The correct pronunciation is right around the corner," she said.

"Guer-tuh."

The crack of thunder startled Hazel. She reached out for Sam's hand.

"That might be it," she said.

57:PM

The cats were arranged like matchsticks, Martha said. She
joked that she wanted to pick the fat calico up, strike it, and
light her cigarette. Emily shut her eyes.

AM:58

Missy had legs, and she knew how to use them. She slid them into jeans or wrapped a skirt around them. She walked with her legs to the grocery store. She used her legs to help haul everything up the stairs and into her kitchen, and she used her legs to walk back into the bedroom and back into bed. It was easy to use her legs, she thought, drifting off.

June continued preparing her apartment for Terrence's visit, even after it became apparent he would not arrive. She arranged the furniture, thinking *Terrence is not going to like this chair* or *I wonder what Terrence will see first* and then she would stand at the entry, letting her eyes fall on the problematic chair, and the carefully arranged photographs, and the strange carved bowl that June loved but knew for a fact that Terrence would not love, and there it was, anchoring the whole of the room together, sticking out like a bruise. It was wood with tarnished metal accents, nothing fancy, something she had found at a secondhand store when she was looking for curtains to hang so that Terrence would not see the metal blinds and think less of her.

It concerned June that she was taking the sentiment too far, but there was a certain enjoyment to be had from preparing the house for a man, for cleaning and waxing the floors with the thought that he would, at any moment, walk up the stairs (in these fantasies, he had his own key), drop his bag on the couch, and touch her casually on both shoulders before stepping around her to open the fridge. June told herself, *This fantasy could be of any man.* This was, in theory, true. But for that night, it was Terrence, and in the morning it would be Terrence, and June tried not to think beyond that.

AM:6Ø

The dog's ears twitched. Simon rubbed scar solution onto the tops of his hands as he had every day for the past six months, trying to erase the marks left by a cooking accident. He had grown accustomed to the scar solution, an elixir of onion peel extract that smelled like the waitress girl at the Italian restaurant when her downy arm brushed his cheek as she leaned over to refill his drink.

Simon stood over the dog on the back porch, surveying the overgrown grass and peach trees and cobwebbed grill that, combined, represented his set of summer projects. He tried to remember the time of day he was born, deciding eventually on five thirty-two in the morning. It was a Presbyterian hospital back then. That was before it was bought and turned into a research center where they studied people with night terrors. Patients woke at all hours, screaming for their mothers. Everybody's got to start somewhere.

61:PM

Dear June,

I want you to know that when I said I would never wash my hands again, I was serious.

Sincerely,
Terrence

AM:62

When you're tangled up with your woman in a bed, it feels right to further tangle yourself.

"I wish I had a hat," Simon said.

"I wish you *were* a hat," Betty said. "I wish you were *my* hat. I would carry you with me, wrapped around my skull, when I was having a bad day. You could protect my image, if you were my hat."

"I would have to be stylish."

"Far be it from you to not be stylish. You would be the envy of all, and of all hats, in the neighborhood. I would go on walks outside, just to show my hat off to the people, and as I passed, there would be some jealousy there."

"We would both be able to sense it?"

Betty pressed her face into Simon's neck. "I would be able to sense it, and you would be able to sense *me*."

63:PM

After a few hours or days, Terrence decided to try out his voice. "Charles," he said.

"Yes, Terrence?"

"I'm afraid we will never escape this box."

"That is certainly the simplest way to articulate that particular fear."

"Charles?"

"Yes?"

"We have fallen out of time. If we die in here, will anyone find us?"

"That calls upon some important questions. Will *we* continue to exist as such, for example. And if we will, is it true that everyone else will—or in fact that *anyone* else will—continue to exist as such, and if that's all true, will the box continue to exist as such. All of these elements have to come together perfectly, and it's somewhat narrowing to assume they will, with or without our contributions."

"Charles."

"What is it?"

"I cannot find the exit."

"Neither can I, old friend. Neither can I."

Of course, the conversation was just starting to get somewhere when a frayed electrical connection sparked and set the gas station on fire.

"We should really, really be going," Emily said. "I'll tell you all about it if you start driving."

Martha shook her head. "I have to start driving to hear about your lack of attraction, then. So as long as it's convenient for you, we'll talk about how you can't look at me."

"I can look at you," Emily said. Her eyes were fixed on the smoke. Employees were hustling patrons through the front doors. One of the customers gestured frantically at them. Emily rolled down her window. "The gas station is about to blow up," the man said.

"You're easily distracted," Martha said. "You can't stop to see the good in people."

"There's plenty good," Emily said, watching the man cross the street.

"You say that now, but you can't even see the good here. Most people die alone yet here we are, together. If you were holding me right while this gas station blew up and took us with it, we couldn't be closer." She placed her hand on Emily's knee.

Emily stared at the hand. "You're insane."

"Let's take it slow," Martha said, reaching for the elastic band on Emily's stocking. Black smoke poured thickly from the windows and doors, from the ventilation hoods on the roof. Emily felt something that wasn't entirely fear.

65:PM

During his time as a hermit, Simon lived upstairs from two newlyweds. They rarely cooked, and when they did, things burned. They made love at two or three in the morning most nights, and then one of them—the girl, Simon imagined—got up and took a shower. He thought of the girl in the shower, all of twenty-three, freshly displaced from her parents' home in Colorado, taking a shower in her downstairs apartment in Texas that she shared with her husband. Simon imagined she lathered her hair with unscented shampoo and repeated the phrase: *My husband.*

AM:66

Through the trees under her window, June could just barely make out the swimming pool. She had never seen anyone in it, but every day, two rottweilers took a lap around it. They loped around casually, not looking for anything in particular. The water shimmered. It was hot outside, and the people who owned the pool would probably be down there enjoying it if they weren't at work, earning money to pay off the pool. June wondered if it was better to be at work, paying off a pool, or at home, watching the dogs run.

67:PM

Carla woke up, still drunk, and surrounded by Supreme Court justices. Ruth Bader Ginsberg was retching in the toilet. Antonin Scalia was wearing Carla's underwear. Senior members of appellate courts were passed out in bizarre positions, splayed across her kitchen floor. She was frightened and disoriented.

She got herself up and ate two gas pills, two sneezing pills, a vitamin pill and a tablespoon of oil and you know what Carla did? She got herself a job.

Frances needed a man she could sink her life into. The perfect man, she observed, would like her but not really enjoy her friends, and the feeling would be mutual. She and her perfect man would eventually stop going to their friends for advice. They would eventually see each other only, and one morning, they would wake up to find that they had fused together, just slightly, at the upper-thigh. The fusion would not be uncomfortable, and would allow for some level of privacy for each. The days of uncertainty, and annoyance, and misunderstanding, would not be entirely over, but whenever such feelings arose, Frances or her perfect man would simply reach to their thigh area and gently pluck the shared skin like a harp string.

69:PM

The insomnia had a calming effect on Reginald, who was accustomed by then to the disappointment of lying awake in bed. At night, small things came to the forefront. The metal cord on the ceiling fan made a rhythmic tapping noise. He made a mental note to pick up a balance kit from the store.

Squirrels ran down their corridors from the attic and into the plumbing behind the bathtub, avoiding the traps Reginald had set for them. The sounds comforted him and kept him awake. If the walls could talk, they would say, *Help! There are squirrels in my brain!*

Those infants have a right to privacy. They may be infants now, tumbling about in their onesies while the rest of us have to work to make a living, but pretty soon they're going to be cogitating, speaking, members of society, and who are you to draw a line in the sandbox between infant rights and human rights?

71:PM

The causeway had an erosion problem and the monument maker had extra stones. The city manager saw an opportunity. At the water's edge, the tombstones made a somber beach. The stones were largely production errors— misspelled names and cracked bevels. A few of the stones belonged to the unlucky deceased who couldn't afford the final payments. Loved ones could visit the watery memorial garden, if they so chose. Most did not.

Are you growing mistrustful of others? Do you suspect your wife does not actually have cancer? Is every trip to the mailbox an exercise in loathing and remorse? Are your coworkers having trouble finding anything interesting to say when they talk about you behind your back? Do you deeply despise people who possess many of the same opinions and motives as your own?

73:PM

Tess wouldn't give everything up for Wallace. She found the sentiment behind that statement to be a little tired, a little oversimplified. She had given things up, but if someone had placed the option in front of her and made it perfectly clear, *you're giving this up for that man*, she would have said, no, I'm not, don't be foolish, I'd give nothing for him when he's given nothing in return. What she didn't know was, love doesn't work like that. It doesn't trade one-for-one. Tess didn't yet know it takes until you have nothing left, until it feels like the blood in your body doesn't have the energy for a whole circuit.

AM:74

Lifting a heavy box of files had injured Carla's back. She sat hunched at her desk, feeling foolish, wondering if old age had finally caught up. Her daughters were grown, and though the men who pursued her did plenty to make her feel like a kid in college, she could see the graying around their temples, the odd areas of slackening skin that matched her own.

75:PM

They all went out together to the railroad tracks to see the funeral train roll by. Martha and Hazel were pushing each other because they were just kids, and they gained a distinct pleasure from standing next to the tracks without getting yelled at, a pleasure which could be best expressed in meanness. Martha pulled one of the pigtails that Hazel spent so long getting even with the other. So Hazel dug her fingers into Martha's arm and Martha squealed and Carla hauled back and smacked the two of them so hard they nearly fell off the backside of the embankment. She looked back at them with an incredible anger that Hazel and Martha would not understand until they were much older.

AM:76

Olivia sees a butter knife on the banister atop the stairs. She fantasizes wildly about the ways in which it might plunge into the ones she loves.

The butter knife makes the entire room feel dangerous. An intruder might not have any desire to stab her until he reached the top of the stairs and felt the butter knife under his hand. Olivia cannot go on until she collects the butter knife and puts it in the sink, where it belongs.

77:PM

Ask yourself: If you were sitting on a girl's couch, and you realized the couch smelled like urine, would your first impulse be to wonder if you were the one who created the urine? Would you feel a sudden sense of guilt, like you didn't belong on the couch at all, and once she came back out of the bathroom, she would take a rolled-up newspaper and swat your ass until you slunk, whimpering, to her open hand? What we're saying here is men are dogs.

To clean a couch, one must first mix an enzyme cleaner with soap, and then use a clean towel or rag to scrub the soapy water into the couch. After a significant amount of cleaning, one then rinses the towel, refills the bucket with hot, clean water, and scrubs anew, removing soap and residue. Depending on the remaining visibility and odor of the stain, another pass may be necessary with soap and rag, water and rag. It may be necessary to pause between treatments, or to allow the soap mixture to soak into the material. What we're saying here is our lives are furniture.

79:PM

"They're gold flakes," Wallace said, reaching to touch them on his back. "Genuine."

Tess held her hand against the textured gold on Wallace's tattoo. She drew her fingers back. "Are not," she said.

"Indeed they are. The artist was fantastic. He literally fused the metal to my skin, and I have to get it retouched every five years."

The gold leaf made a pattern of fish scales across his lower spine.

"It's beautiful," she said.

"You're beautiful," he said, turning his head halfway.

"Not as beautiful as a gold flake."

He considered it. "Maybe not. It was a very special process."

"Must have been," Tess said. She felt sure she would die alone.

AM:8Ø

Good morning, John Mayer Concert Tee! You seem to have weathered the past few days rather poorly. Your cuffs are split, you're stained at the neck. The graceful visage of The One Who Will Play the Smooth Guitar is sullied by dirt scrub and bent into a permanent, unnatural shape. You are rigor mortis in clothing form, John Mayer Concert Tee. You accept the elements, the wearer and all his flaws, and your reward is a cramped place in the crack of a window, keeping out the morning sun. You understand what it means to suffer, and what it means to bestow grace. You understand the ditch and the sewage and the long night.

81:PM

The yoga instructor declared they were pushing toxins out of the body. As the sweat dripped from her face, Chastity licked it to see if it tasted any more toxic than usual. It did not, so she considered the possibility of airborne toxins, or toxins without a discernable taste, toxins that could seep from the body unannounced, and land on the floor, invisible to the naked eye, waiting to be picked up by bare feet, like a splinter, and re-absorbed.

AM:82

Why does the rain make us feel so romantic and strange? Maybe it's the fact that we are unnatural spectators of it, from inside our homes, and it is a reminder that we have the power to live our whole lives like this, if we choose. It's not the smell of fertile ground kicked up by raindrops, or the slick leaves, or the way we must amplify our voices to be heard over this larger presence. It's the power of the rooftop that makes us want to fuck under it.

83:PM

Not a hundred feet from camp, Reginald found two stumps next to each other, like twins. He liked the look of them and sat on one, propping his rifle up against the other. It was early yet and the bugles hadn't sounded, though dew had already wet the tall grass enough to soak the cuffs of his jeans. He didn't have regulation wool like most of the other reenactors. He spent some time rolling up the jeans until he could see a line of hair from over his crew socks.

He tapped his pack of cigarettes. The others rolled their smokes by hand and lit them with antique lighters. Reginald was there because his friends convinced him to come. They said he could maybe meet some of the women who came to reenact war nurses. Olivia must have told them to say that, which embarrassed him. Most of the war nurses were fat, anyway. The fact annoyed Reginald more, though he was also fat and smoked too much.

He lit his cigarette with a lime-green lighter and thought about how he would save the furniture store.

Pressing on in the winter makes more sense. There's snow, and when you press on through the snow, you can feel it and sense the difficulty. During the summer, it's dry land for months. Maybe a little ocean water, but that's hardly pressing on. Hell, that's a vacation.

85:PM

Before the storm, Hazel had washed the sheets and stretched them across the mattress while they were still damp. Sam moved from side to side with some discomfort.

"I feel like we wet the bed," he said.

"I feel like a brand new bitch," Hazel said. Her eyes were still closed. He didn't know what to make of it. At that moment, he didn't even want to touch her. He felt a distinct fear that she might either disappear or stay the same.

June kept the windows open the first few weeks, but got annoyed at sweeping up all of the dead houseflies, closed the windows, and switched on the air. She still kept the shutters open for a while, but started closing them at night because she couldn't gauge the tree cover under the dining room window, and she kept feeling like the neighbors were standing in their backyard, watching.

Sometimes she forgot to open the shutters again during the day, and the lack of sunlight made her sleepy. She started opening her eyes only halfway, and then not opening them at all unless she needed them to make chicken salad or sweep the floor.

Eventually, chicken salad grew less important. The chicken straight out of the can gained its own intricacies, and adding mayonnaise and celery and bread and cheese seemed like too much. She could find the chicken in the pantry without opening her eyes, and soon enough, she learned to find the trash can to dispose of the can without peeking even once. She was a high-wire artist. Her invisible audience watched from their backyards.

87:PM

The trap in the attic was catching some seriously large squirrels. Rats too, but Reginald didn't want to frighten Olivia by telling her there were rats crawling up through the walls. He installed a humane trap, a kill trap, and a poison trap, and left it up to the vermin to make the choice for themselves.

AM:88

Carla realized that there are morning people and evening people, and she was both of those, but what she certainly was not was an afternoon person. Words came harder. Things got unpleasantly bright while she dulled, squinting at the computer screen, sipping espresso and making a conscious effort to not eat too much, to not lie down, to take the phone calls and be patient, most of all, be patient.

89:PM

Reginald sat on the pile of mattresses and wondered how his wife's friends would die. One particularly dependent woman would be the most likely to be involved in a jealousy-driven murder. Another was a bad driver and too sensitive about it. Still another had undiagnosed health problems. The moon above the loading dock was almost full and Reginald watched it, trying to determine in the stillness if it was waxing or waning.

For a while, Carla dated a man named The Amazing Chet who guessed people's weight at the science museum. The Amazing Chet was his real name, given to him by his mother. Twenty years before he had traveled with a circus. The science museum liked the novelty and The Amazing Chet was very good, guessing within the half-pound, and exactly more often than not. He used to sit at a folding table and write the weight down on a note card for the person, but the exhibit grew in popularity and the science museum made a special booth for him, with electronic output so that, when a patron stepped on the platform, he could enter their weight and have it be digitally displayed above their head. The Amazing Chet's exhibit became the most popular in the museum, and scientists of various disciplines came to record and study his accuracy.

The Amazing Chet would come home, tired but happy, and lift Carla in the air to greet her. "You've dropped three ounces since yesterday," he would say. "Are you drinking enough water?"

Eventually his divining career grew too important, and the science museum gathered the funds to turn him into a traveling exhibit. They hosted a gallery party to kick off the tour, and The Amazing Chet invited all his old friends from the circus. Carla was surprised to see so many people. The Amazing Chet was a dull man, in her eyes.

91:PM

When cold and warm fronts meet, at the right velocity and temperature, a hurricane forms. Tess remembered the morning of the hurricane seventeen years before. That afternoon, she watched the blue sky and white clouds from her seat on the bus and strained to feel something in the air. Seventeen years later, she felt her loneliness rise up to meet an overpowering urge and suppressed the desire to board the windows.

"Being with you is like a plate of hair," Andrew said. "A dainty bone china plate, covered in hair. And everyone at the table is watching me and waiting to see if I'm going to eat it."

Carla looked at him and yawned. "Being with you," she said, "is like taking a sleeping pill."

93:PM

Is there too much suffering in the world, and not enough philosophy, or is it the other way around?

Press your right side to massage your ascending colon. Press your left side to massage your descending colon. Express the toxins you are able to express, and ignore the others.

Control the impulse to check the locks on your door.

AM:94

The more bleach in the bedsheets, the greater Chastity's impulse to roll around in them. A party would be thrown, she decided, the kind that would tell a small story in the contents of the dustpan the next morning. Detached sequins and mint leaves muddled by high heels, shrimp tails mixed in with a few shards of broken glass, a crust of bread. She rolled in her bleached sheets until they wrapped about her like a storm, and she fell asleep in the eye of it.

95:PM

A man cultivates a terrible feeling in the woman who loves him. He turns the feeling of love on itself. The woman sees what love looks like in its grotesque selfishness. The price of her knowledge? An enthusiastic event, and another, and the actor will watch herself doing terrible things.

The girls were doing yoga in the living room. Missy played some calming spiritual music and lit a candle.

Chastity winced, feeling the wood floor under her thin mat. "I want the kind of man who goes looking for a war," she said.

Missy aligned her hips up and back for Downward-Facing Dog. "There's a few wars out there already," she said. "Should be easy to find."

"Not a real war," Chastity said, after her third attempt at the Plow. "Nothing that would kill him."

"What, you just want things that will make him stronger?" Missy exhaled through her nose and stood up. "Boring."

"I want him to find something worth fighting for every day."

"This, coming from the woman with the most dangerous party theory ever." Missy raised her arms and took a deep breath. "I guess I could have seen it coming," she said, exhaling.

Chastity felt it wasn't a true party until something got broken and someone got hurt. "I want a man who knows what it means to fight," she said.

"Slap a pair of skates on the girl and you've got a roller derby," said Missy.

97:PM

Hazel constantly felt the need to express something inside of her. With age, she would learn that everyone has that same feeling, and that the need to express comes from a sensible desire for community, but that reasonable people either forget the feeling or get tired of talking about it, as when all the gossip about an embarrassing acquaintance finally winds its way down and the friends stare at each other across the table, each thinking, *now what.*

Martha was face down on the bed with her feet draped over the closed violin case as if she was having them examined. She didn't move when Emily walked in and sat next to her.

"I thought I'd join a bluegrass band," Martha said. Her words were muffled by the pillow.

"You practiced?"

"I can play the songs, but it makes me nervous. Everything makes me nervous."

"It's normal to be nervous." Emily rested her palm on the bottom of Martha's left foot.

"Great," Martha said, "I'm nervous and I'm *normal*." She started to cry.

"Do you even like bluegrass music?" Emily asked.

Martha blew her nose in the center of the pillow. "I'll wash it," she said. "There's just that feeling, you know? When something happens, and you have to let it happen and you get *that feeling*, like your heart is breaking? That's how I feel about joining a bluegrass band."

"I didn't know you liked bluegrass music."

Martha rolled onto her back. Her mascara had smeared into two dark smudges on her eyelids. It made her look like an animal with its fur or feather patterned like false eyes. "That's just it," Martha said, closing her real eyes and inadvertently widening the false ones. Emily could barely watch.

99:PM

Olivia's whole body shook, not like a leaf but like the tree itself, a deep kind of shudder that only happened at the hands of loggers. A tree feels its deepest movement in those final seconds. She once watched a program on television where a falling tree snapped at the trunk, creating a ten-foot-long catapult that tossed a logger fifty feet into the air. They called it kickback.

AM:100

Betty and Simon drove down the dirt road playing Amish or Vietnamish.

"A Bible in every compartment," he said.

"A compartment in every Bible," she said. "Tet Offensive."

"Non-offensive. What's mine is yours."

"What mines? Agent Orange."

"Orange preserves." He tapped his fingers on the steering wheel. "I Am Become Jebediah, Raiser of Barns."

Betty leaned back and closed her eyes. "Good one."

1Ø1:PM

Goosebumps came more easily, though it was the middle of the summer. Tess sat in front of the fan and alternated between jerking sobs and laughter at the sound she made. That hiccup of breath was a terrible sound to hear in the dark, and she would laugh, rub her goosebumps down, and sob. She needed to make the decision to cut, because making the decision would bring instant pain and healing simultaneously. She was the kind of girl who climbed the tallest tree and cried to be let down, but she was also the kind of girl who would scramble and jump down on her own as soon as someone went in for the ladder. Here in the dark, she needed to decide.

AM:1Ø2

Missy looked at her watch, and back at Chet. "Half an hour," she said. She was sitting cross-legged on his chair, naked, watching him on his bed.

Chet yawned. "Until when?"

"It's been half an hour since I felt good about this situation."

"The sex?" He wondered when she might finally leave.

"This whole situation. It's been about thirty-two minutes."

"I don't know what I'm supposed to do about it," he said, pressing his palms to his eyes for a second before removing them and blinking in the light. He was tired, he wanted sleep. "It was your idea, as I recall."

"Don't give me that. It was our idea, together."

"You essentially teased me until I gave in."

"You gave in. Fantastic." She rolled onto the floor and covered her breasts with a phone book. "Now I'm a rapist, and a bad lay."

"Jesus, Missy, you're not a rapist."

"I teased you, you gave in. You gave in like it was prom night." She moved the phone book over her face. Chet reached to the side table for his glasses, which he polished carefully before placing them on his face. He looked at her breasts. Behind the phone book, she was crying.

"Don't be dramatic," he said.

"Time keeps going," she said. "I thought it might not, but it did."

Missy was making some kind of extended moan from behind the phone book. Chet watched her chest heave. The phone book bobbed up and down with her breath.

"We didn't go to prom together," he said.

1Ø3:PM

Frances's pale skin felt stretched so thin that if she scratched her face or arms, she would mangle herself. She imagined the skin would peel up underneath her fingernails like lacquer from a table. Perhaps she wasn't drinking enough water, she thought, perhaps she was sleeping too much again. When she slept, she had wonderful dreams.

AM:1Ø4

And the angels looked upon the land, and they said, LORD, look upon this woman who waxes her stairs at seven in the morning. And the LORD looked upon the earth with grave mercy and spoke, saying: That woman must perish, for she is well and truly mad. And the woman upon the earth slipped on her waxen stair and cracked two ribs and suffered a skull fracture on the way down and she looked to the heavens and with her dying breath said, Why, LORD? And the angels did open beers and laugh, and the LORD did take pleasure in the morning.

1Ø5:PM

Terrence realized his eyes were closed. He wasn't sure how long they had been closed or if he had been sleeping during that time. Perhaps five feet away, he heard Charles moving across the floor of the box. Terrence coughed and Charles stopped moving.

"Terrence?" Charles asked. "Are you awake, old friend?"

"I think so."

"You may have been meditating. I wouldn't want to disturb you."

"What are you doing over there?"

The noise and movement began again. "I'm tamping down this velvet material," Charles said. "I was feeling a little buoyed."

"That was your imagination."

"It was an uncomfortable feeling. There wasn't much better to do, while you were meditating."

Terrence felt the kernel of an argument in Charles's tone and it immediately made him nervous, though they were friends. Perhaps it was the confined space, Terrence decided. He closed his eyes and tried not to stir again, or to be bothered by the velvet noise.

There's no rule saying you have to be a child to compete in the Westbrook Elementary School Science Fair! I read the Rules and Regulations very closely! I spent approximately twenty-two hours on my volcano, which I have named Carla! I put her chemicals in bottles I labeled with my calligraphy pen! When I arrived, holding Carla aloft, the women at the check-in desk admired my work aloud and asked me who I was bringing this project in for and I said I am entering this category for myself, please! My name is Leonard and this is Carla! And they did laugh and one of the women made a clicking noise with her fingernails on the table because she wouldn't recognize ambition if it slapped her in the face!

1Ø7:PM

Reginald fought the impulse to help Betty sign the loan. She had the paper wedged awkwardly under her left arm, still holding a wine glass as she attempted with her other hand to manipulate the pen into action. *There's no reason to rush*, he said to himself, *she'll get it on her own*. It was essential, as a salesman, to not be too pushy.

She wasn't putting enough pressure on the pen to start the ink flowing. She shook the pen gently and looked at her husband. Reginald thought about the importance of the ink that was at that moment trapped in the reservoir of Betty's pen, a very nice Cross fountain, now that he looked at it, with some kind of filigree along the side, possibly an inscription. Perhaps it once belonged to her father, a man who in his day would run circles around Reginald's rinky-dink furniture store. Quite possibly, the pen was the only item of his she carried around, though it seemed equally likely that her purse was full of tie clips and cufflinks and miniature portraits of the man. Just one stone from one cufflink could get Reginald out of the mess he had gotten himself into. He prayed for a few inches of ink.

Starting a family is easy: The sign said "Free Kittens," and Sam pulled the car over. Two fat people, a man and a woman, sat in lawn chairs behind a cardboard box. They had positioned themselves at the side exit of the Wal-Mart, where Sam and Hazel had just been stealing light bulbs.

The trick to stealing light bulbs is to walk in with an empty light bulb carton. Wave the carton at the greeters so they can see it, and then take what you need. Hazel would sometimes wave to the greeters on the way out, the full carton in her hand. The more blatant, the better, when it comes to stealing.

"Free light bulbs, free kittens," Sam said. "Today's our lucky day."

"Today's your lucky day!" the fat woman parroted. She flipped open one of the cardboard flaps and hauled out a kitten.

"They're real pretty," the fat man said. He was drinking from a juice box.

Hazel reached for the gray and white kitten and touched its paw. "Do those kittens have six toes?"

The woman nodded. "This kitten could shake your hand," she said.

"That's a sign of a good kitten," Hazel said.

The woman looked a little offended. "They're free," she said, thrusting the kitten towards Hazel. "There's four more."

"We'll take them all," Sam said. And they did.

1Ø9:PM

Tess kept a secret: her left hand was turning into a claw. She felt the tendons tightening up in her forearm the week before, and had written it off as the onset of carpal tunnel, but the tendons continued to tighten. The feeling spread into her hand, which began to curve like a scythe, the bones lengthening a little and then bending, almost imperceptibly, until her fingers hardened into one immobile point and her left hand was fully a claw.

Tess kept the secret, but compensated by repeating it to herself. She would lie in bed, curled around her left hand, holding it gently to her knees. *My hand is a claw. My hand is a claw.*

AM:11∅

June woke up covered in seeds. They were small, toasted sesame seeds, thousands of them all over her body. She had never been covered in seeds before and it was a strange feeling, like a snake might feel in sand. There was no explanation, as far as she could see, for the sudden appearance of all the seeds. It was a comforting feeling, and June turned over three times in the slippery weightlessness before falling back asleep.

111:PM

They were in love! Carla wore her hair up and Andrew saw everything as a sign. They spent an entire afternoon sitting side by side in a coffee shop, taking more meaning than necessary from the world around them. A man wearing boxing gloves walked down the sidewalk in front of them and they took that to mean they would be together forever.

AM:112

Good morning, John Mayer Concert Tee! It has been a while. I'm feeling a need to overstress my happiness at seeing you, hanging on the laundry line between my house and the neighbor girl's house. It's one of those mornings where everything is tinged with miracle. The waxed floor is a miracle! The dirty dishes are a miracle! The day ahead is a gift from heaven. This isn't to say I'm happy, John Mayer Concert Tee, but you are a miracle. If we mated, John Mayer Concert Tee, our children would have jersey-knit skin. They would never speak unless spoken to, and even then they might not speak. But they would be soft, and they would smell like fabric softener, and they would love us, and we would love them.

113:PM

"I just had a terrible dream," Martha said.

Emily turned to look at her. "You were sleeping?"

Martha flicked on the turn signal, changed lanes. "I dreamt we were in a awful car accident," she said.

"I was just thinking the same thing."

It wasn't that much of a coincidence, really, as they were weaving through late-night traffic. It bothered Emily more to think that Martha had been asleep at the wheel, though surely it was just an expression.

"It was a bad dream," Martha said. "We were in an accident, and I was okay."

"Did I have a bar through my head?"

Martha shook her head and blinked. Emily realized she was staring.

"You weren't okay," Martha said.

"I'm okay now," Emily said, turning to look out the window again. Without looking back, she reached across the seat divider, found Martha's hand, and held it.

Betty cracked the crust of her crème brûlée with the edge of her spoon. "This is a symbol of my love for you," she said.

"You've said that about a lot of things," Simon said. "You said that about the entrée as well. And the bottle of wine."

"It's all true," she said. "Your cup of coffee is a symbol of my love for you. This spoon. Our waiter. The ceiling. Your fingernails. The crack in that windowpane. The cars parked outside. My shoes. Your shoes. The pastry chef. This tablecloth."

"What about the flowers?" he asked, gesturing to the buds in a vase between them.

She looked at him. "Don't be stupid," she said.

115:PM

Frances ate fish at all meals. In the morning, when the newspaper came, she ate a bagel with lox. Mid-day, she would prefer something light, like tuna in olive oil, but at night she would make cod fried with polenta, rich seafood stews, baked salmon, seared tuna rolled in pepper and sea salt. She declared that she would eat fish until the day she died, and then she would eat fish as an angel.

As the days went on, her fish consumption grew simpler. She ate fish as a singular pursuit. She ate alone, with her back to the door, the fish alone on a plate, without spices or sauces. She stopped cooking rice and vegetables. She drank a glass of water before the fish and a glass of bourbon after. She ate the fish from a white plate, and the fish was white against the plate. When the fish was gone, she licked the white plate.

When Missy or Chastity called, Frances talked about her day in relation to fish.

She would say, "I just ate some fish," or "I am about to cook some fish, broil it perhaps."

Her friends silently wondered when they would be invited for dinner, and then they began to wonder it aloud, but she never had a solid answer for them.

She would say, "I'm sorry, I only defrosted enough fish for one."

When her friends pressed her to make future plans, Frances seemed confused. Her friends decided she was demurring and stopped calling, because they were all sensitive people. She was sensitive, too, and didn't understand why they stopped calling.

Carla snapped the tines off the plastic fork with her thumb. "No matter how deeply I bury you in the gravel pit of my memory," she said, "you come crawling back out."

"There's no need for poetry," Andrew said. "I'm just here for my chair."

"I'm eating," she said.

"You just broke your fork."

"See, Andrew, that's just how you are. It's no damn business of yours how I eat, and what I eat with. What if I brought this fork to the door just to show you how serious I am?"

"All I'm saying is, you're not eating right now, and I want my chair back."

"I want those years back," Carla said. "I want my youth back."

"You may have your youth," Andrew said. He had a bag with him, and he reached into the bag and pulled out a small, carved box. He handed it to her and she held it with both hands.

"Sorry I kept it for so long," Andrew said.

Carla took a step back to let him in. "Your chair is in the kitchen," she said.

Terrence and Leonard grew up in Dallas and moved to different cities at the same time. They were bored with Dallas. All the women in Dallas were preternaturally interested in the fact that they were twins, though they were grown by then and had exhausted all avenues for conversation regarding their twinship.

Of course, luck would have it that the woman Terrence was starting to feel comfortable around would squeal and hold her palms together when she learned he was a twin.

"Who's older?" June asked, resting her chin on her upturned palms. It was the most excited she'd been all evening, even after he told his humorous stories from his job at the collections agency.

"He is, by thirteen minutes." Terrence couldn't stop fussing with a dollop of glitter glue on the Formica table between them. He was trying to edge his fingernail under it.

"What did your mother do in that thirteen minutes?" June asked. "Have a cigarette? Wonder, 'is this second one really worth it'?"

Terrence laughed politely. "Right," he said, answering none of the questions. June had no way of knowing that his mother was long dead, and she seemed nice enough that she would have been embarrassed if he mentioned it.

"Anyway," June said. Saying "anyway" was a conversational tic of hers, it seemed, as she had resorted to it three times over the course of an hour.

Missy shrugged. "What I want to know is," she said, dropping her fork into a puddle of maple syrup, "why does everyone keep talking about how fat Frances is?"

"Who's Frances?" Chet asked. Missy and Chet had been married for six months.

"Oh my God," said Chastity, at that moment breastfeeding her three-year-old son. "Frances is so plump."

"She's plump!" Missy said. "Exactly! She's pleasantly plump. I mean, there but for the grace of God go the rest of us." She pinched the thin layer of fat on her own belly.

Chastity made a face. "I'll never be that plump," she said, shifting her weight. The boy toothed her nipple and she winced.

"Not as long as you keep up that tit lipo," Missy said, mostly for the benefit of Chet, who hadn't stopped staring since Chastity unbuttoned her blouse and hauled it out.

Missy plunged her fork into the last square of her french toast, swirling it around and thinking of all the opportunities for pain she had missed in her life. "Frances is so fat," she said, satisfied.

119:PM

They found Tess in the center of her living room with her legs folded neatly under her. The pose suggested that she had received sudden and shocking news, and had to sit down immediately to allow her body to catch up with the emotional significance.

The rope hung loose from the rafters, still on her neck, its frayed ends spun out behind her like a child's toy. The shoe on the table, five feet from the girl, suggested that she swung about eight horizontal feet before the rope broke. You could imagine the look on her face.

AM:120

One day, everyone stopped over-thinking. We started thinking just as much as we should, and not any more than necessary. There were no more misunderstandings whatsoever. Minor disagreements were forgotten, not turned into proof of larger things. Trivial errors of speech or judgment were just as important as items on the breakfast menu: you chose waffles and I chose eggs and it was a god damn miracle.

121:PM

Carla stepped out of the dressing room and took a modest turn. "How do I look?" she asked.

Hazel looked at her mother with a critical eye. The knot halter cut of the gown revealed her slender shoulders. The vibrant pink, which had looked a little young on the rack, added color to the woman's face. Carla looked in the mirror, put one bare foot forward, wiggled her hips a little.

"Mom," Hazel said, "you look like a brand new bitch."

"Well that's fine," her mother said. "I somewhat feel like a brand new bitch."

Charles was painting the ceiling red after the landlord specifically told him not to paint anything at all.

From the door, Doreen looked up at him. "It must take a special kind of stubborn," she said, "to live your life."

"It will look incredible," he said, stretching his arms overhead. He winced in the stretch.

"You should get off that ladder."

"It all has to be done at once, or it won't appear even."

"You'll pull a muscle in your back and we'll starve."

"You want to do it?" he asked, waving the roller at her. Red paint dripped to the drop cloth below. At least he had the foresight to put down the drop cloth, she thought.

"I don't want you to do it," she said. "The landlord doesn't want you to do it. Nobody wants you to do what you're doing right now."

"It will look incredible. The baby will love it."

"What baby?"

He looked at her, exasperated. "For God's sake, woman. I'm simply thinking ahead."

123:PM

Olivia couldn't bear to watch them take the rest of the tree. The men propped ladders up against the trunks and climbed up to stand at eye-level with her office. She shut the blinds and shuddered as branches fell against the walls and windows. When she opened the blinds again, she saw that the tree central to her viewing area had been compromised, swarms of gnats attending to sap glistening on the cut trunk. The tree bent back unnaturally from the window, as if shamed. She realized the hatred she felt for the people and things over which she had no control.

They sniped at each other quietly outside the changing room at the department store. "Everything makes sense if you think about it long enough," Missy said. "That's your problem."

"Now, that makes sense," said Chet. "I bet you thought about that for a long time."

"Does this make me look fat?"

Chet looked appraisingly at his wife. "You gained half a pound this week."

"For Christ's sake."

"Maybe a quarter pound," he lied.

"You make all that stuff up anyway. I can't understand why those scientists call you amazing."

She flounced back into the changing room. Chet took a seat by the doorway.

125:PM

"Terrence," Charles said. "Friend."

"Charles?"

Charles mumbled something, but Terrence could barely hear Charles's voice from the other side of the box.

Terrence leaned forward. "What's that?"

"Infants are smarter than we think," Charles said, faintly.

"Infants?"

"Infants," Charles said, "are smarter than we think."

"You're all right, Charles?"

"They're smarter," Charles said.

Wallace's concept of honor ensured he would never go to sleep satisfied. His concept of God was that a being that creates bread from bread is to be feared. Love is intensity with less spectrum, sadness is spectrum with less intensity. Wallace believed in the horizontal nature of pain and the verticality of love.

127:PM

The children found the cube, and shrieked over it as children do. The adults couldn't be pulled away from the picnic at first, and assumed that the children had found a shed snakeskin or a gopher hole during their exploration of the causeway. Only when the kid touched the monolith and burned his hand did the parents come running, attracted by the screams.

It was an iron cube, ten feet high and wavering like a mirage. The Thurber kid wept bitterly, his hand already swelling with the blister.

Nobody knew what to make of the thing. It was too big to have been carted in on a pickup truck. It might have fit on the open bed of an eighteen-wheeler, but there were no tire marks in the area, no damaged vegetation and not even a road nearby wide enough for a load that size. It was as if the block had been cast in its spot and destined to remain. And then there was the issue of the inscription.

They didn't notice it at first, between the screaming kid and Betty Thurber's wailing panic, hustling him back to the car for ice, and the pandemonium of parents finding their own children and clasping them to their chests and lifting them up at once. The object in question itself received little scrutiny. Only when the women took the children back for calamine lotion and jelly beans did the men notice the printed text, sized no larger than a half inch, on the shady side of the block:

EVERYTHING MUST EVENTUALLY SINK.

AM:128

The tour bus slowed to a halt and the occupants took up their cameras, craning their necks.

The young, pretty tour guide switched on her microphone. "On your left," she said, gesturing to a modest brownstone, "you will find where the philosopher lives."

An audible gasp rose among the crowd. Shutters clicked and mothers hauled their children up to see.

"He lives there," an older woman said in a daze. "He solves our problems there."

The pretty tour guide recited her memorized notes with reverence. "The philosopher is the wellspring from which our lives flow. Without him, there would be no heaven and hell, no love or feeling or meaning. The philosopher toils in silence, alone, a thankless life. Perhaps we will catch a glimpse of him today."

The crowd leaned forward, eagerly scanning the windows for movement. Perhaps the philosopher would peer out the window as he drank his morning coffee, or sit on the stoop and have a cigarette.

They watched. Nothing happened. The driver released the air brakes with a hiss and continued down the street.

129:PM

Try not to fill yourself with anxiety. Take your pills on time. Consider the proper way of doing things. Parcel your week into a series of days, your day into a series of hours, your hour into a series of thoughts. Know when to push yourself and others. Congratulate yourself for small successes to mask the other growing pile. There has been a ladder in your office for weeks now, and you're trying to be polite about it.

June believed in spells that could be broken, and in making the final push. She wrote letters to congressmen and companies and strangers. Her life's goal was that people understand her, and each other, and themselves. It was the only kind thing she did.

131:PM

Olivia coughed when she heard him pick up the line. "Reginald," she said.

"You're drunk."

"You took all my money, Reginald."

"We talked about this. Jesus Christ, we had an arrangement. I was going to work it out."

"*Your* Jesus Christ," she said, examining with one eye the contents of her wine glass. "You took my friends' money, too. You relied on my connections to ruin my God-dammed standing among my own friends."

"Wash your face and take a shower."

"Why would I take a shower when I could take a *bath*?"

He sat right down on the floor. "I'm not playing a game with you."

She tossed her glass overhand and it smashed merrily against the wall. "You always play the game," she said. "We're not playing any more games."

"Got it," he said.

"I don't think you do," she said, hanging up.

This funny-smelling couch is a symbol of my love for you.
This mechanical litterbox is a symbol of my love for you.
This interesting pen is a symbol of my love for you.
This wooden floor is a symbol of my love for you.
This year of loneliness is a symbol of my love for you.
This concert tee is a symbol of my love for you.
This glass of water is a symbol of my love for you.

133:PM

Emily picked up the violin and played. Her back pained her, had pained her all day, and now Martha's violin only made it worse. She felt the sweet strains of paranoia drifting back. They told her to look over her shoulder, and when she did, they told her to check the lock on the door, and when she did that, they told her that her fears had meaning and depth, and that she was right to feel them. Each shadow meant something different and strange, an unfamiliar animal or a line of weapons. These visions were terrifying, but after they went away, she felt a strange kind of peace that those things existed in the world, that her world was powerful enough to conjure them. *My world*, she thought.

acknowledgments

Many thanks are owed to Sam Axelrod, Justin Boyle, Zach Dodson, Jonathan Messinger, Stacey Swann, Michael Wolfe, and my parents. Grateful acknowledgment is additionally made to the editors of the publications in which these stories first appeared: *American Short Fiction, Jettison Quarterly, The M Review, Take The Handle*, and *Wigleaf*.

about the author

Amelia Gray is a writer living in Austin, TX. Her writing has appeared in *The Onion*, *American Short Fiction*, *McSweeney's Internet Tendency*, *DIAGRAM*, and *Caketrain*, among others. Her work has been chosen as the finalist for *McSweeney's* Amanda Davis Highwire Contest and the *DIAGRAM* Innovative Fiction Contest. She received an MFA from Texas State University in San Marcos.

featherproof BOOKS

Available at bookstores everywhere, and direct from Chicago, Illinois at

www.featherproof.com

Printed in the USA
CPSIA information can be obtained
at www.ICGtesting.com
LVHW012332090823
754786LV00001B/46